THE OFFICIAL

QUEENS PARK RANGERS

ANNUAL 2025

Written by Francis Atkinson and Matt Webb
Designed by Mathew Whittles

A Grange Publication

© 2024. Published by Grange Communications Ltd., Edinburgh, under licence from Queens Park Rangers. Printed in the EU.

Photographs © Rex Features

ISBN 978-1-915879-92-9

CONTENTS

FRESH START
NEW LOOK

QPR'S new home kit for the 2024/25 campaign was revealed for the first time when we played Leeds United at MATRADE Loftus Road in our final home fixture of the '23/24 season.

The classic home shirts from the 1960s and 1970s are mirrored in this new design while, for the very first time, three shades of blue are incorporated in each blue hoop, as well as on the cuffs.

The shirt retains the popular, state of the art Ti-Energy 3.0 fabric, with the addition of strategically placed panels in an alternate fabric for extra breathability. These factors combine to produce a shirt which, at first glance, is pleasingly traditional while also containing the positive aspects of modern design and fabric technology.

Fabrizio Taddei, head of pro clubs development for Erreà, said: "As we look forward to our ninth season with the R's, we wanted to bring something new to the

2024/25 shirt by adding a subtle, tonal grading to the blue hoops.

"We have also added a new twist to the more traditional round neck, which as well as providing added detail, also gives additional flexibility to the collar.

"We hope that everyone connected with QPR feels the same way as we do about the new design."

Our 2024/25 home kit is now on sale in store and online – as are our brand new range of goalkeeper shirts.

Sported by summer signing Paul Nardi, the jerseys use the coveted Ti-Energy fabric, but also a new pattern.

Our home goalkeeper shirt is a bold maroon and our alternate third kit is green for the new season. The sky blue away 'keeper shirt featured last season when Rangers beat Leeds 4-0 in W12.

All three shirts are coordinated in the same style, with tonal panels and an intricate tone-on-tone design across the chest, in three different colours. Possibly the most striking of these is the rich maroon with logos in gold, followed by a light sky blue for contrast and finishing with one for the traditionalists in green with crisp white printing.

These performance shirts are also extremely comfortable, for both goalkeepers and fans, and the colours provide something for everyone.

In line with gambling advertising and sponsorship regulations, CopyBet's logo is not present on junior replica kits.

PAUL NARDI

STAN BOWLES

PUTTING QPR ON THE MAP

Following the sad passing of arguably Rangers' greatest-ever player earlier this year, Chris Guy pays a special tribute to 'Stan the Man'...

The number 10 shirt became synonymous with our club in the mid-1960s thanks to Rodney Marsh. He helped put Rangers on the footballing map between 1966 and 1972 as back-to-back promotions in 1967 and 1968 took us from Division Three to the top flight, alongside winning the League Cup final in March 1967.

At that stage Rodney was arguably the most important and beloved player in our history, when he was sold to Manchester City in March 1972 it was thought, understandably, that he was impossible to replace.

A month later, the next chapter of the Queens Park Rangers number 10 story would begin. It was the penultimate home game of the 1971/72 season with Carlisle United the visitors, less than 8,000 fans braved the rain but were rewarded with a 3-0 home win.

Despite their defeat, one player stood out for the opposition that day, a skillful long-haired number 10 called Stanley Bowles.

Stan impressed manager Gordon Jago so much on that rainy afternoon that five months later, he agreed to pay Carlisle a reported £112,000 (a then-club record) and Stan headed south.

Stan, who admitted he was incredibly nervous in the days leading up to the match as he was worried about the fans' reaction, made his debut in a Second Division match against Nottingham Forest. He couldn't have made a better start.

On two minutes, he crossed from the left for Don Givens to give the R's the lead. Half an hour later Stan would score the first of his 96 Rangers goals with a header, he celebrated in style with a backward somersault.

Rangers went on to win 3-0 and the Loft had found a new hero in the number 10 shirt.

Two weeks later Stan would show a wider audience his unbelievable talent by scoring against Cardiff City, highlights of the game were shown the following day on LWT's 'The Big Match' programme. Stan's goal in the 3-0 win was one of the finalists for the programme's goal of the season competition.

Stan's total of 17 goals in 35 league games were a massive part in Rangers' promotion to the top flight at the end of the 1972/73 season.

This included his first hat-trick in a 5-0 demolition of Swindon Town, he also scored twice in both games against 1973 FA Cup winners Sunderland.

August 1973 saw Stan on the stage his talents deserved, the top tier of English football.

For the first time in the club's history, we had a player performing at the top of his game at the pinnacle of English football. Rodney Marsh's chances were limited due to injury in our previous season in the First Division.

There were so many magical Stanley memories from the 1973/74 season – the brace scored at Wolverhampton Wanderers in a 4-2 win, his nonchalant finish in a win over Arsenal, outperforming the great George Best by scoring twice in a 3-0 win over Manchester United on New Year's Day 1974.

Not forgetting of course giving Ron 'Chopper' Harris the runaround by scoring twice in a 3-3 draw at Chelsea, that having scored the goal that knocked them out of the FA Cup a month earlier, as well as scoring in

the league game at Loftus Road earlier in the season.

Stan was rewarded for this fine form with three full England caps at the tail end of that season. In a Home International match in Cardiff in May, Stan scored his first (and only) England goal in a 2-0 win.

Three days later, however, an emotional and angry Stan would walk out on the England squad after being substituted during a match against Northern Ireland at Wembley. It was a time of turmoil at his club as well with manager Gordon Jago resigning in that same month.

Jago was persuaded to return but matters came to a head two months into the 1974/75 season with Jago, the man responsible for bringing Stan to W12, leaving the club.

On the pitch this didn't affect Stan too much, he scored a televised brace at Arsenal in a draw at Highbury under caretaker manager Stan Anderson.

Stan was often at his best when provoked, this proved to be the case on this October afternoon, responding to the jibes of the Gunners' World Cup-winning midfielder Alan Ball.

By the time of the next game, at home to Liverpool, a new man was in charge, a manager who would take the club and Stan on to a whole new level, Dave Sexton.

Stan would click immediately under the former Chelsea boss, scoring in four consecutive matches in November.

It wasn't all sunshine and roses, though, with Stan

not happy at all at being substituted in an FA Cup fifth-round defeat at West Ham, caught in full by the TV cameras.

Stan had a special relationship with chairman Jim Gregory, who would do a great job of dealing with Stan's numerous transfer requests (which must be a club record in isolation!).

Stan's friendship with team-mate Don Shanks was the stuff of legend, the duo would often team up and drive secretary Ron Phillips mad with requests for a sub before wages day. Ron even resorted to climbing out of his office window to avoid the pair.

The pair were inseparable, enjoying their nights out at the local White City dog track. Don was a true lifelong friend to Stan, going as far as running the New York Marathon in 2018 at the age of 66 to raise money for the Alzheimer's Society following Stan's diagnosis.

Inspired by watching the great Dutch and German sides, Dave Sexton had Rangers playing in a continental style not seen regularly in England at the time.

The 1975/76 opening-day win over Liverpool in W12 set the tone for the season, a week later Rangers hammered reigning champions Derby County 5-1 on their own turf. Stan scored a hat-trick.

The local Derby newspaper were glowing in their praise of Stan – "the delicacy of his ball control created havoc in the Rams' defence".

As has been well documented, the '75/76 season is arguably the greatest in the history of the club. Rangers finished their 42-game league campaign top of the table.

In a situation that would never happen today, Liverpool were allowed to play their final game at Wolves 10 days after our campaign had finished.

With many travelling R's fans in attendance, the Reds won 3-1 to pip us to the title.

But our second-place finish meant that European football would come to W12 for the first time in our history.

The stage was perfect for our Stanley, during our UEFA Cup campaign he would break the record for goals scored by a British player in a European campaign – Stan netted 11

goals. This tally included two hat-tricks against Brann Bergen of Norway and two goals in Bratislava against a Slovan side featuring many of the Czech team that had won the European Championships only months earlier.

This 3-3 draw is regarded by many as the greatest away performance in the club's history.

The footage available of Stan from the 1976/77 season shows him at his absolute best. His jink past the Cologne defence to break the goalscoring record in the UEFA Cup and his superb run and finish against Sunderland are two fine examples.

His excellent form in domestic and European football earned Stan a recall to the England squad, he won his fourth cap in a World Cup qualifier in Rome in November 1976 and his fifth and final cap in a friendly against Holland at Wembley in February 1977.

However, in March 1977 Stan would suffer a broken leg in a match at Bristol City. He showed incredible resilience in rehabbing the injury and he was back in the team for the first match of the 1977/78 season.

That match at Bristol was the last game that Stan would play under Dave Sexton, who left for

Manchester United that summer.

Under new manager Frank Sibley, Stan was deployed in a more withdrawn midfield role as the team came to terms with the long-term absence of Gerry Francis. It was a season of struggle following the departures of Frank McLintock, Dave Webb and Dave Thomas, a lot was expected of our talisman in his new role.

Stan produced some magical moments despite the struggles, with the winner against Arsenal at Loftus Road and brilliance in the mud in a 6-1 FA Cup fourth-round replay win over West Ham United.

After narrowly avoiding relegation, Frank Sibley left his role and was replaced by former coach Steve Burtenshaw for the 1978/79 season.

This was another tough campaign that ended in relegation for Rangers. Stan was dropped by Burtenshaw and accused the manager of, "making me a scapegoat for recent results".

In May 1979, Stan would have another new boss in W12 and his final one in Tommy Docherty.

The relationship between the two colourful characters was always going to be an interesting one. Stan, as candid as ever, upset the 'Doc' at the pre-season team photo by telling the assembled media that we had, "no chance of promotion".

Stan wasn't pleased that Docherty then took his treasured number 10 shirt from him, Paul Goddard, Billy Hamilton, Tony Currie and his old mate Don Shanks wore it in the early part of the 1979/80 season. The R's faithful had to get used to seeing their idol sporting the number seven shirt.

Stan's seven-year association was coming to an end in W12, the relationship with Docherty wasn't helping.

Stan's final Loftus Road goal, just like his first, was a header in a 4-0 win over Charlton Athletic. His 96th and final QPR goal was captured for posterity by the TV cameras in a defeat at Cambridge United.

A dribble past a couple of defenders and a chip into the top left-hand corner with his right foot, it was apt that he jumped into the arms of his old mate Don Shanks in celebration.

Stan was signed by Nottingham Forest in December 1979 by another of the game's great characters in Brian Clough.

Stanley Bowles is arguably the greatest player in the history of Queens Park Rangers. He joined us when the morale of fans was at a low following the sale of Rodney Marsh. He took us to a whole new level with his breathtaking skills on some of the game's biggest stages.

Stan was born in Collyhurst, Greater Manchester but truly became one of us – so much so that Brian Clough would refer to him mistakenly as a 'cockney'.

Stan embraced everything about life in W12 and the fans loved him for it, during his playing days he would be seen in the local bookies, cafes and of course at the White City dog track.

Despite his reputation for off-field activities by some, many of his peers would often say that he was a dedicated trainer with an immense will to win.

Stan was a regular in the west London area even after his playing days, it's fair to say that as well as being one of our greatest-ever players he was also the most accessible.

He was a regular in the pubs around W12. He never seemed to be a big drinker, he just loved to be around the fans that adored him.

He would never refuse an autograph or a photograph, despite being swamped by fans at times.

Stan played the game purely for enjoyment, as he said himself; "When I played, I just played. I didn't think about it. I found it easy".

It's this attitude that made him so popular with our fans, other former players have blotted their copybook with negative comments about the club over the years.

Stan never did this, he always said nothing but positive things about the club, the fans and west London.

As the great man said, "My seven years at QPR mean more to me than my time at all my other clubs put together".

We are all so grateful that we had those seven years, thank you Stanley for giving us so many happy memories, he truly did put us on the map.

Many fans say even now that Stan is the reason that they support the club, many have even named their sons after him.

It's fair to say that Stan is arguably the best and most loved player in the history of Queens Park Rangers Football Club.

The bond that was created between Stan and our fans will last for eternity. His goals, skills and exploits will continue to be passed down from generation to generation of our fans.

Rest in peace, Stan. Gone but never, ever forgotten.

25
Lucas
ANDERSEN

Midfielder

Denmark

TICK THEM OFF! ✓

WE'VE mapped out QPR's 2024/25 Sky Bet Championship opponents.

The line-up includes Luton Town, Burnley and Sheffield United – who were all demoted from the Premier League last term.

Similarly, also competing at this level for '24/25 are Portsmouth, Derby County and Oxford United following their respective promotions from League One.

How many of our opponents will you be visiting this season? Tick them off as you go and jot down how many away games you attended at the end of the campaign!

Away games

- [ ] Sheffield United
- [ ] Luton Town
- [ ] Sheffield Wednesday
- [ ] Blackburn Rovers
- [ ] Derby County
- [ ] Burnley
- [ ] Leeds United
- [ ] Cardiff City
- [ ] Watford
- [ ] Bristol City
- [ ] Swansea City
- [ ] Norwich City
- [ ] Plymouth Argyle
- [ ] Hull City
- [ ] Millwall
- [ ] Coventry City
- [ ] Portsmouth
- [ ] West Brom
- [ ] Middlesbrough
- [ ] Stoke City
- [ ] Oxford United
- [ ] Preston North End
- [ ] Sunderland

MY AWAY GAMES TOTAL:

BACK TO BLACK

QPR'S new 2024/25 away shirt was released in late June – the stylish black jersey features gold embellishment on the logo and sponsors, alongside red, gold and green trim around the cuff and collar.

The colour combination creates a striking shirt which is both smart and fashionable.

A closer look at the sleeves reveals a subtle, tonal pattern of symbols which have been taken from the QPR club badge of 1953-72 – the crest of the borough of Hammersmith – reminding us to always look forward but never forget your roots.

The '24/25 away shirt – first worn during our pre-season fixtures in Girona, Spain – has a dual-fabric construction, including Erreà's celebrated Ti-Energy 3.0 fabric which creates additional comfort.

The shirt is paired with matching black shorts and socks, both of which also have gold, red and green detailing. Like the shirt, the shorts have a small section of the tonal symbols.

GOING FOR GOLD

We also have a third kit for the 2024/25 campaign – debuted during our pre-season fixture against Tottenham Hotspur in W12.

This stunning new strip is prominently gold with black trim, and features both gold shorts and socks.

Similar to the away jersey, there is a subtle acknowledgement to the QPR club badge of 1953-72 – the crest of the borough of Hammersmith.

The coat of arms from the crest is recreated on the front of the shirt in a tonal effect.

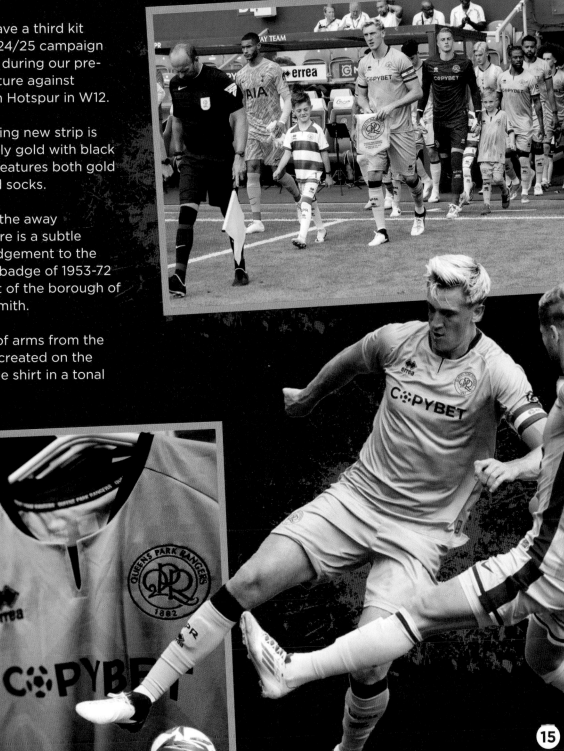

NINE NEWBIES

QPR moved to sign a total of nine new first team players during the summer transfer window.

Meet our new recruits for the 2024/25 Sky Bet Championship campaign...

1 PAUL NARDI

Rangers' first signing of the summer, goalkeeper Paul Nardi joined QPR following the expiry of his contract with Belgian top-flight side Gent.

The 30-year-old stopper began his career in France with Nancy before moving to Monaco in 2014. He enjoyed loan spells with Stade Rennais and Belgian side Cercle Brugge before completing a permanent switch to Lorient in 2019.

After three years with the French side, which included promotion to Ligue 1 in his first season, Nardi moved to Gent and now he is relishing the next chapter of his career.

"I am really excited to discover this new club, this big club," he said.

"I have followed a lot of the Premier League and the Championship since I was young so when I heard QPR had a big interest in me, it was an easy choice for me."

Nardi, a former France Under-21 international, believes he has made big strides in recent seasons and is eager to show his capabilities with the R's, explaining: "In the last three or four years I feel my goalkeeping is the best it has been. But now moving to a new division, I have to work a lot every day to be the best."

Nardi, who made seven appearances in the Europa Conference League during his time with Gent, is also looking forward to experiencing the atmosphere in W12, adding: "I am so excited to discover Loftus Road.

"I will do my best in my new shirt."

② HEVERTTON SANTOS & ③ LIAM MORRISON

Defensive duo Hevertton Santos and centre-half Liam Morrison arrived in W12 in early July.

Full-back Santos, 23, joined the club after leaving Estrela da Amadora in the Portuguese top flight, having come through the youth system at Sporting Lisbon.

"I am very happy to be here," he said.

"This is a very historical club with a huge story. I am really excited to be with the fans at Loftus Road and to feel their passion."

Having spent his career in Portugal, Santos wants to test himself in a new environment, explaining: "I like this type of challenge. Life is made of opportunities and this is a big one for me.

"It was always my dream to play in England because I love the way you think about football here, the way you play football here. When you compare with other countries, it is like another sport."

Santos, who played 29 of 34 league games in the Primeira Liga last season, added: "Last year was a nice experience for all of us, it was special for me. Playing in the big stadiums of Portugal against Sporting, Benfica, Porto, it was very good."

Describing himself as a player, Santos said: "I like to be active on the attacks, I like to do assists and goals, create plays for the team.

"I have pace, and in defence I am strong in the duels and one-v-ones. I enjoy both sides of the game.

"In modern football, you have to be complete and that is what I am looking to be – that complete player."

Meanwhile, centre-half Morrison, 21, signed permanently from Bayern Munich. The Scotland Under-21 captain came through the ranks at Celtic before moving to the German giants in 2019 and spent last season on loan at Wigan Athletic in League One.

"I'm delighted," he said. "It has been something that has been in the works for the last couple of weeks and I am really looking forward to getting started."

Having spent the past year with the Latics, where he made 35 appearances in all competitions, Morrison feels he is well-equipped to deal with the challenges the Championship will throw at him, explaining: "League One is also a demanding league, a very physical league. There are a lot of games, like the Championship.

"I know the Championship is a step up but I am confident I will be able to handle that step."

Having spent the past five years with Bayern Munich, Morrison explained why he was keen on a move to W12.

"The way QPR are aiming to progress in the future is something that suits me," he said, "and the way they love to play football is also my style of football, so for me to take the next step in my career, this was a no-brainer."

Describing himself as a player, Morrison said: "I am a typical Scottish defender – you throw your body in front of the ball to make sure it doesn't go in the goal!

"I am comfortable with the ball at my feet, a lot of my game is about playing out from the back, and I have good leadership qualities so hopefully I can bring that to the team."

4 ŽAN CELAR

Striker Žan Celar joined QPR from FC Lugano, signing for an undisclosed fee.

The 25-year-old arrived W12 on the back of three hugely successful seasons in the Swiss top flight, where he netted 40 goals in 95 appearances.

Celar, who was the top scorer in the Super League last season, said: "I am very excited.

"I can't wait to start, join the team, join my new team-mates, start training and start matches."

The Slovenia international is looking forward to his first taste of English football and is confident he will be able to handle the transition to the Championship.

"I think I will adapt well," said Celar, who made 52 appearances for club and country last season.

"I know there are a lot of games but I like to play games, so I can't wait.

"The next step now is important for me and I think this is the right place. I will try to do what I have been doing and hopefully I can help the team with my goals."

Despite playing less than three weeks ago in the Euros against Portugal, Celar is already keen to get back on the grass.

"I have had enough of a rest," he said. "I am very excited to start training and to start matches with my new team-mates."

5 JONATHAN VARANE

Jonathan Varane completed a permanent transfer to QPR for an undisclosed fee, joining from Sporting Gijón.

The 22-year-old midfielder, who came through at French side Lens before joining Sporting two years ago, is looking forward to the prospect of playing in England with QPR.

"I am very happy and excited to be joining this historic club," he said.

"I think for my career this is a good step and I am excited to meet my new team-mates, join the group and start with the club.

"I know the style of QPR and I think for me it is a good move to continue my career here."

Varane, who made 25 appearances in all competitions for the Spanish second-tier side last season, described himself as a player, explaining: "I like to defend, I like winning balls, giving passes and progressing with the ball on the ground.

"I think the Championship will be very good for me."

Varane had been training with Sporting so arrived eager to get going with the R's, adding: "I am going to give 100% for the club, my team-mates and the coach.

"I want to complete the objectives of the club and I will give all I can to do it.

"This is a dream for me so I can't wait."

6 KOKI SAITO
& 7 KADER DEMBÉLÉ

QPR completed the loan signings of attacking midfielders Koki Saito and Karamoko Dembélé in mid-August.

Saito joined for the duration of the 2024/25 campaign while Dembélé moved to W12 on an initial season-long loan.

Saito, primarily a left winger, arrived from Belgian outfit Lommel. The 23-year-old had been on loan at Sparta Rotterdam for the past two years and was a key part of the Eredivisie side.

"I am really looking forward to playing for a big club like QPR, and I want to contribute to the team by providing results, goals and assists," he said.

"Thinking about where I want to be and what I want to achieve, it will be a great step to play for QPR."

Saito, who represented Japan at the Paris Olympics, added: "Dribbling is one of my strengths. But also creating chances and running behind the defenders that leads into goals and assists are also the strengths I have."

Dembélé joined the R's from French Ligue 1 side Brest. The 21-year-old, who plays on the right wing but can also play as a No.10, came through the ranks at Celtic in his native Scotland before moving to France two years ago.

Last season he impressed during a loan spell with Blackpool, picking up the players' player, supporters' player and young supporters' player of the year awards for the League One side.

Now he is looking forward to the next stage of his development with QPR.

"I am really excited," he said. "I have heard amazing things about it here and I just can't wait to get started, to be honest.

"This is a great platform for me to progress in my career. I spoke to Martí [Cifuentes] and I spoke to Christian [Nourry] and I really felt the 'want', which I think is important.

"The conversations I had with them were good and from there, my decision was made."

Dembélé made 47 appearances for the Tangerines last season, scoring nine goals and providing 14 assists, and he believes that game time has been vital for his development.

"That was the most important thing at that stage of my career," he said. "I hadn't had a lot of games before that so I am really grateful to Blackpool for giving me that opportunity. I am hoping to build on that this season."

(8) NICOLAS MADSEN

Nicolas Madsen completed a permanent transfer to QPR from Belgian top-flight side KVC Westerlo.

The 24-year-old central midfielder joined for an undisclosed fee.

Madsen came through the youth system of FC Midtylland in his native Denmark before a loan spell with Herenveen in the Dutch top flight in 2021/22.

He had been with Westerlo for the past two years and is now relishing plying his trade in England with QPR.

"I am excited," he said. "The league excites me and the club's project excites me a lot.

"I can see me developing and that is why I am here."

Madsen, who has represented Denmark at Under-17, U18, U19 and U21 level, stands 6'4 tall and he admits that makes him quite unusual as a player who likes to have the ball at his feet.

"I am a very technical player even though I am also quite tall," he said, "so it may be a little unusual but with the ball I have my best abilities."

Madsen has shown his versatility in recent years in the centre of the park, and that culminated in him scoring 14 goals from midfield last season to be Westerlo's top goalscorer.

"Last season I played as a 6, 8 and 10, and it gives me the flexibility to perform in all these positions," he said. "If I could choose, I would play as an 8.

"With the role I had last year, I was playing a bit more offensive and I got into these situations I like, to create chances and also score goals."

Madsen arrived in west London ready to play, having made four appearances in the Belgian top flight this season.

"I am in the best shape I have ever been in," he said.

"Always the best way to get going at a new place is to get started fast and play some games.

"I am excited also to see the fans and the atmosphere in the stadium."

⑨ HARRISON ASHBY

Our final signing of the summer window, Harrison Ashby joined QPR on loan from Newcastle United.

The 22-year-old right back will remain in W12 for the duration of the 2024/25 season.

Ashby, who came through the ranks at West Ham United before moving to St. James' Park in January 2023, is relishing the opportunity to progress his career in west London.

"There is only one place that I wanted to come and I am really excited for what's ahead," Ashby said.

"The people I spoke to, and the chats that we had, straight away my head turned."

Explaining why QPR felt the right fit, Ashby admitted how Rangers play their football was a key factor.

"I am a very attacking full-back so the style of football suits me," he said.

"A big thing coming on loan is the style of football you are going to play. When you are on loan you want to improve, you want to get better and help the team.

"The setup here, I can definitely improve my game."

Ashby has represented Scotland at Under-17 and Under-21 level and is excited to play in the Championship again, having spent last season on loan at Swansea City.

"The experiences I have been though have really helped me in my career and coming here is another experience I can add to the list," he said.

"Now that I am here and I have seen around, my head is fully turned to playing for QPR and getting started."

THE STANLEY BOWLES STAND

10

Ilias Chair

Midfielder

Morocco

1

Paul
Nardi

Goalkeeper

France

23

CASE FOR THE DEFENCE

Centre-half pairing Steve Cook and Jake Clarke-Salter were the big winners of QPR's 2023/24 End Of Season Awards.

Cook was voted Supporters' Player of the Year for the campaign. The summer signing's displays alongside Clarke-Salter played a big part in Rangers' revival last term.

Clarke-Salter was voted Ray Jones Players' Player of the Year.

Sinclair Armstrong picked up the Daphne Biggs Young Player of the Year award for a second successive season, while Jimmy Dunne's incredible late winner against Birmingham City in W12 was your Kiyan Prince Goal of the Season.

Dunne was named Achilleus Security Junior Hoops Player of the Year.

Fans were able to select their NNR QPR FC Women's Player of the Year, too, with top scorer Grace Stanley once again picking up the award.

CLARKE-SALTER

DUNNE

COOK

Jimmy Dunne and Jo Blodgett were our PFA Community Champions of the Year for supporting numerous club and Community Trust events and projects.

Finally, Anuj Bhardwaj was named Supporter of the Year – as voted by fellow fans.

Anuj followed the team both home and away last season, offering travel to supporters in his eight-seater bus at no cost. He works at Heathrow and continues to transport international fans to home fixtures from the airport on matchdays.

STANLEY

ROLL OF HONOUR

Supporters' Player of the Year

Steve Cook

Runner-Up: Sam Field

Ray Jones Players' Player of the Year

Jake Clarke-Salter

Runner-Up: Kenneth Paal

Daphne Biggs Supporters' Young Player of the Year

Sinclair Armstrong

Runner-Up: Rayan Kolli

Achilleus Security Junior Hoops Player of the Year

Jimmy Dunne

Runner-Up: Steve Cook

Kiyan Prince Goal of the Season

Jimmy Dunne

v Birmingham City (H)

Runner-Up: Andre Dozzell v Middlesbrough (A)

NNR QPR FC Women's Player of the Year

Grace Stanley

Runner-Up: Zoe Cohen

PFA Men's Community Champion of the Year

Jimmy Dunne

PFA Women's Community Champion of the Year

Jo Blodgett

Supporter of the Year
Anuj Bhardwaj

FOCUS ON
ELIJAH
DIXON-BONNER

NATIONALITY
England

POSITION
Midfielder

MARRIED
No

CHILDREN
No

CAR
Mercedes

FAVOURITE TV PROGRAMME
Breaking Bad

FAVOURITE PLAYER IN WORLD FOOTBALL

Kevin De Bruyne

MOST PROMISING TEAM-MATE

Rayan Kolli

FAVOURITE 'OTHER' TEAM

Liverpool

CHILDHOOD FOOTBALLING HERO

Steven Gerrard

FAVOURITE SPORT OTHER THAN FOOTBALL

Tennis

MOST DIFFICULT OPPONENT SO FAR (PLAYER)

Barry Bannan – he's a very good player

MOST MEMORABLE MATCH OF YOUR CAREER

Making my debut in the FA Cup for Liverpool

BIGGEST DISAPPOINTMENT SO FAR

No regrets!

FAVOURITE MEAL

Oxtail with rice and coleslaw

FAVOURITE HOLIDAY DESTINATION

Jamaica

FAVOURITE PERSONALITY (IE COMEDIAN, ACTOR)

Dave Chappelle

FAVOURITE ACTIVITY ON DAY OFF

Going for brunch with my sisters

FAVOURITE MUSICIAN / BAND

Drake

POST-MATCH ROUTINE

I love to grab a pizza!

BEST FRIEND IN FOOTBALL

Folarin Balogun, Monaco

BIGGEST CAREER INFLUENCE

My dad

PERSONAL LIFE AMBITION

To be a good man

IF YOU WEREN'T A FOOTBALLER, WHAT WOULD YOU BE

Movie star!

PERSON IN WORLD YOU'D MOST LIKE TO MEET

Can I pick three?! I'm going to say Julia Roberts, Leonardo DiCaprio and Michael Jordan

NET BUSTERS

While QPR's 2023/24 campaign certainly wasn't all smooth sailing, there were still a number of impressive goals scored – be it thanks to individual excellence or tidy team work. Here's the pick of the bunch, including the Kiyan Prince Goal of the Season – as voted for by R's fans...

JACK COLBACK
vs SOUTHAMPTON (A)
26 August 2023

Rangers ran the eventually-promoted Saints extremely close on the South Coast and should have left with more to show for their efforts than a 2-1 defeat.

Colback, on his first start for the R's, equalised on 32 minutes. Paul Smyth's industry down the right eventually resulted in the ball deflecting back into the path of the former Nottingham Forest midfielder 25 yards from goal, who subsequently arrowed a low effort in off the inside of the post.

Goals from Sam Edozie and Adam Armstrong ultimately undid the Hoops.

ANDRE DOZZELL
vs MIDDLESBROUGH (A)
2 September 2023

Our second victory of the campaign at the start of September saw Rangers win 2-0 at Middlesbrough. Rangers took the lead shortly before half-time – and how!

Ilias Chair and Colback exchanged passes just short of the penalty area before freeing Andre Dozzell 25 yards from goal, who subsequently hammered home an unstoppable effort via the left-hand post.

Colback completed the scoring after half-time.

LYNDON DYKES
vs SWANSEA CITY (H)
19 September 2023

Lyndon Dykes came from the bench to grab a late, late leveller for QPR, who drew 1-1 with Swansea City at Loftus Road.

After Josh Ginnelly's contentious seventh-minute opener gave the visitors the lead, it looked like Swansea may come away from the capital with all three points as Rangers – despite plenty of industry – struggled to work opposing goalkeeper Carl Rushworth.

Dykes had other ideas, though, meeting Ilias Chair's cross with a powerful header in the 92nd minute to earn Gareth Ainsworth's charges a point.

ILIAS CHAIR
vs ROTHERHAM UNITED (A)
4 November 2023

Ilias Chair netted his first goal of the season as Martí Cifuentes' tenure as head coach began with a 1-1 draw versus Rotherham United.

Ken Paal's clever pass down the left freed Chair, who cut inside to hammer the ball into the top right-hand corner.

The R's were pegged back in the 70th minute as Rotherham's Georgie Kelly came from the bench to touch home Cafu's free-kick from deep.

LYNDON DYKES
vs STOKE CITY (H)
28 November 2023

Lyndon Dykes was at the double in an important 4-2 win over Stoke in late November – our first at home for the season – with his second goal particularly impressive.

The definition of a topsy-turvy affair, Lyndon's 11th-minute penalty put Rangers ahead, before the visitors turned the game on its head through Ryan Mmaee and Wouter Burger.

But the R's roared back, kickstarted by Dykes' impressive second goal of the night. Chris Willock's right-flank centre deflected up into the path of the Scotland number nine in the box who, on the turn, produced a stylish finish into the bottom left-hand corner.

The R's earned all three points thanks to Ben Pearson's own goal and Willock's stoppage-time strike.

NET BUSTERS

CHRIS WILLOCK vs HULL CITY (H)
9 December 2023

Goals from Willock and Chair earned QPR a 2-0 victory over Hull City – Rangers' third on the bounce in the Sky Bet Championship.

A thoroughly-entertaining affair throughout, Willock's stunning effort moments before half-time set the Super Hoops on their way in W12. Patient approach play from the Hoops ended with the attacker taking possession of the ball before sending a delicious effort past Ryan Allsop and into the top right-hand corner from 20 yards.

Martí's men rubberstamped their win 17 minutes from time. Substitute Sinclair Armstrong's closing down earned Willock the opportunity to turn provider, as his low cross was turned home by Chair on 12 yards.

CHRIS WILLOCK vs ROTHERHAM UNITED (H)
24 February 2024

In February, Rangers came from behind to beat Rotherham United 2-1 and move out of the Championship relegation zone for the first time since September.

In another tense W12 affair, QPR fell behind in just the seventh minute when Tom Eaves finished beyond Asmir Begović at the Loft End. But Cifuentes' Hoops hit back in the second half to climb out of the bottom three on goal difference.

Willock played a starring role – laying on half-time sub Smyth to equalise in the 61st minute. He then got in on the scoring act 15 minutes from time, firing home from 20 yards after combining with Chair to give the R's a huge win in the capital.

SINCLAIR ARMSTRONG vs LEICESTER CITY (A)
2 March 2024

QPR toppled Sky Bet Championship leaders Leicester City to collect a third straight win in our battle to beat the drop.

On a remarkable afternoon at the King Power Stadium, Rangers – who displayed incredible defensive resilience throughout – took a 38th-minute lead through Chair. Substitute Armstrong doubled that advantage when he thrashed home on 57 minutes, only a minute after his introduction.

Ben Nelson pulled a goal back for Leicester on the hour mark to set up an expected nervous finale. But Rangers – backed superbly by 3,000 travelling fans – held on to claim another hugely-important win in the fight for survival.

JIMMY DUNNE
vs BIRMINGHAM CITY (H)
WINNER
29 March 2024

Jimmy Dunne's sensational stoppage-time winner saw QPR come from behind to beat Birmingham City in W12 and move four points clear of the Sky Bet Championship relegation zone.

A highly-charged affair throughout, Juninho Bacuna gave the visitors a 62nd-minute lead following a first half where both sides had their chances to score.

But Rangers battled back to claim three hugely-important points in the fight for survival. Steve Cook put Cifuentes' Hoops on level terms just three minutes after falling behind.

Then, in the second of the six additional minutes, a ball forward was contested by Armstrong before dropping into the path of a venturing Dunne who, from 20 yards, controlled it with his chest before thundering the ball past John Ruddy with his weaker left foot at the Loft End to spark wild scenes of celebration.

STEVE COOK
vs SWANSEA CITY (A)
1 April 2024

Fans' player of the year Cook scored his second goal in as many games as QPR moved six points clear of the relegation zone in the Championship with a 1-0 victory over Swansea City.

Following the last-gasp victory over Birmingham City, Cifuentes' men made it back-to-back wins over the Easter weekend to further strengthen our chances of survival last term – a feat we ultimately achieved, of course.

Cook's 71st-minute effort was the difference in South Wales, hammering home in front of the Hoops' travelling army of supporters following a well-worked corner routine involving both Andersen and Dunne.

SEE ALL THE
GOALS HERE

6

Jake
Clarke-Salter

Defender

England

18

Žan
Celar

Forward

Slovenia

SIGN 'EM UP!

How many autographs from QPR's 2024/25 squad can you obtain?

ALFIE LLOYD

ALFIE TUCK

JAKE CLARKE-SALTER

DANIEL BENNIE

ELIJAH DIXON-BONNER

HEVERTTON SANTOS

ILIAS CHAIR

JACK COLBACK

JIMMY DUNNE

JOE WALSH

JONATHAN VARANE

KENNETH PAAL

LIAM MORRISON

LORENT TALLA

LUCAS ANDERSEN

MATTEO SALAMON

KARAMOKO DEMBÉLÉ

MICHAEL FREY

MORGAN FOX

PAUL NARDI

PAUL SMYTH

RAYAN KOLLI

KOKI SAITO

SAM FIELD

HARRISON ASHBY

STEVE COOK

ŽAN CELAR

NICOLAS MADSEN

FOCUS ON
MICHAEL FREY

NATIONALITY

Switzerland

POSITION

Striker

MARRIED

Yes

CHILDREN

Not yet!

CAR

Uber is my friend currently!

FAVOURITE TV PROGRAMME

Any sport documentary

FAVOURITE PLAYER IN WORLD FOOTBALL

Erling Haaland

MOST PROMISING TEAM-MATE

Alfie Tuck

FAVOURITE 'OTHER' TEAM

Growing up it was Bayern Munich

CHILDHOOD FOOTBALLING HERO

Zinedine Zidane

FAVOURITE SPORT OTHER THAN FOOTBALL

Tennis

MOST DIFFICULT OPPONENT SO FAR (PLAYER)

I played with him, but Martin Škrtel in training

MOST MEMORABLE MATCH OF YOUR CAREER

Two games – I scored five goals for Antwerp v Standard Liège, then scoring a goal for FC Zürich when we won a cup Final. I grew up living next to the stadium

BIGGEST DISAPPOINTMENT SO FAR

Injuries

FAVOURITE MEAL

Anything with Swiss cheese!

FAVOURITE HOLIDAY DESTINATION

In the Swiss mountains or Turkey

FAVOURITE PERSONALITY (IE COMEDIAN, ACTOR)

Muhammad Ali or Vincent van Gogh

FAVOURITE ACTIVITY ON DAY OFF

Spending time with my wife

FAVOURITE MUSICIAN / BAND

I grew up listening to Simon & Garfunkel because my dad was a big fan, The Beatles also

POST-MATCH ROUTINE

Anything that helps me to switch off

BEST FRIEND IN FOOTBALL

Marco Bürki

BIGGEST CAREER INFLUENCE

My former agent who is now sporting director at FC Zürich – Miloš Malenović

PERSONAL LIFE AMBITION

To strive for the best until the end

IF YOU WEREN'T A FOOTBALLER, WHAT WOULD YOU BE

Artist! I like to draw and paint, I went to art school. Or working with my dad as a gardener!

PERSON IN WORLD YOU'D MOST LIKE TO MEET

I would like to talk to Zlatan Ibrahimović

WORDSEARCH

See if you can find all of these well-known football terms hidden within the wordsearch. Good luck!

S	E	L	N	I	W	O	R	H	T	L	L	S	K
L	D	O	V	E	R	H	E	A	D	K	I	C	K
I	I	C	E	O	A	A	R	E	N	R	O	C	R
D	S	L	H	I	G	H	P	R	E	S	S	O	I
I	N	Y	T	L	A	N	E	P	A	L	D	Y	T
N	O	E	S	L	O	W	B	L	O	C	K	E	O
G	V	R	F	C	P	V	R	L	K	D	D	L	C
T	W	O	F	R	R	R	K	U	K	I	E	B	R
A	L	E	L	G	E	D	L	O	K	S	D	B	E
C	Y	L	L	L	R	E	C	F	G	S	I	I	D
K	N	O	L	B	E	N	K	P	E	E	S	R	C
L	I	L	N	O	D	Y	C	I	D	N	F	D	A
E	Y	R	E	D	A	E	H	E	C	T	F	R	R
D	R	A	C	W	O	L	L	E	Y	K	O	S	D

OFFSIDE	DRIBBLE	CORNER
VOLLEY	FOUL	THROW IN
OVERHEAD KICK	RED CARD	ONSIDE
FREE KICK	YELLOW CARD	LOW BLOCK
SLIDING TACKLE	DISSENT	HIGH PRESS
HEADER	PENALTY	

Answers on **page 60**

WHO AM I?

Can you name the QPR players by associating them with the statements listed below?

1

- I began my career at Arsenal
- I made my professional debut for Liverpool
- My QPR bow came in a home fixture versus Birmingham in March 2023

2

- France, Turkey, Belgium and Germany are among the countries I have played professional football in
- I joined the R's from Royal Antwerp in early 2024
- I scored my first Hoops goal the following month, versus Norwich

3

- I learned my footballing trade at Manchester United
- Hearts are among the clubs I have featured on loan for previously
- Sean Dyche was my manager before I made the move to W12

4

- I am QPR's longest-serving player
- Belgium has been home but I represent a different nation internationally
- I have been on loan at Stevenage previously

5

- I made my league debut for Gillingham
- Loans spells at the likes of Accrington, Maidenhead and Dorking have helped ready me for first-team football
- My first-ever league start for the R's came at Coventry in May 2024

Answers on **page 60**

SPOT THE DIFFERENCE

Can you spot the ten differences in the below pictures from when Rangers took on Sheffield United in August?

Answers on **page 60**

IT'S A NUMBERS GAME

Guess these mathematical equations by adding together the shirt numbers of the following QPR players...

Paul Nardi + Joe Walsh =

Jimmy Dunne + Jack Colback =

Steve Cook + Harrison Ashby =

Kader Dembélé + Paul Smyth =

Sam Field + Koki Saito =

Michael Frey + Liam Morrison =

Kenneth Paal + Žan Celar =

Lucas Andersen + Elijah Dixon-Bonner =

Alfie Lloyd + Hevertton Santos =

Jake Clarke-Salter + Jonathan Varane =

Answers on **page 60**

4

Jack
Colback

Midfielder

England

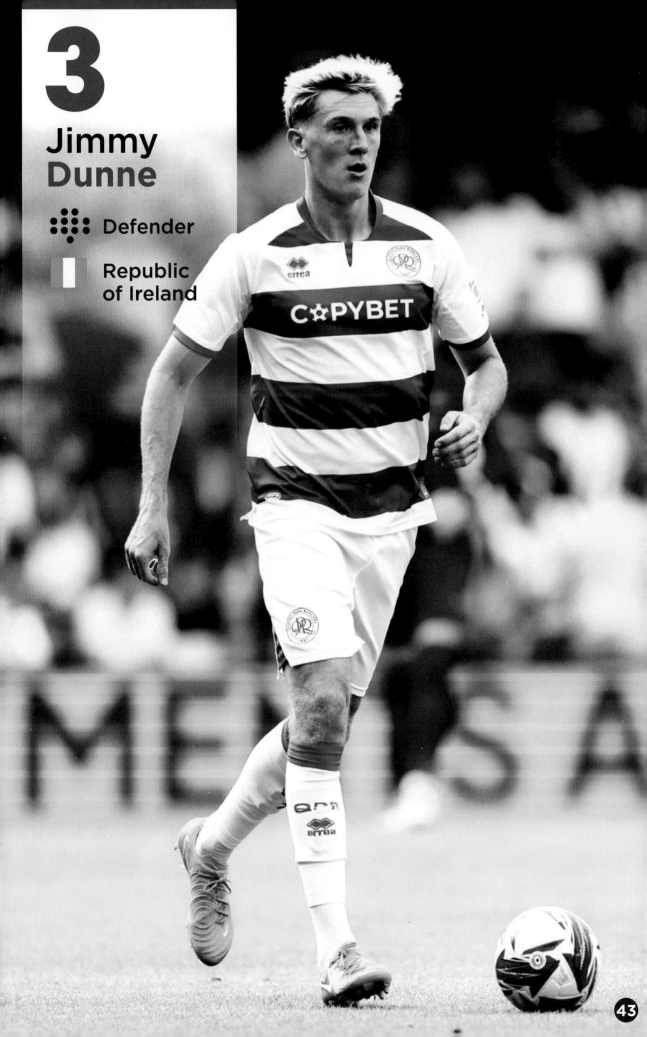

3

Jimmy Dunne

Defender

Republic of Ireland

FOCUS ON
PAUL
NARDI

■ **NATIONALITY**

France

■ **POSITION**

Goalkeeper

■ **MARRIED**

Yes

■ **CHILDREN**

Yes

■ **CAR**

Mercedes

■ **FAVOURITE TV PROGRAMME**

It's a fun show in France – Touche pas à mon poste!

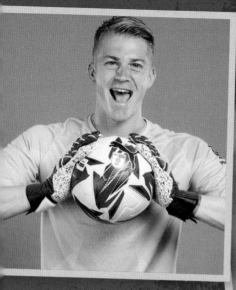

■ FAVOURITE PLAYER IN WORLD FOOTBALL

Gianluigi Buffon

■ MOST PROMISING TEAM-MATE

Matteo Salamon – but we have many promising young players

■ FAVOURITE 'OTHER' TEAM

Nancy

■ CHILDHOOD FOOTBALLING HERO

Hugo Lloris

■ FAVOURITE SPORT OTHER THAN FOOTBALL

Tennis

■ MOST DIFFICULT OPPONENT SO FAR (PLAYER)

Lionel Messi

■ MOST MEMORABLE MATCH OF YOUR CAREER

I remember playing for Cercle Brugge against Genk in Belgium. They won the league but we beat them – it was my day!

■ BIGGEST DISAPPOINTMENT SO FAR

Getting injured last season

■ FAVOURITE MEAL

Kefta with eggs

■ FAVOURITE HOLIDAY DESTINATION

Tanzania

■ FAVOURITE PERSONALITY (IE COMEDIAN, ACTOR)

Jake Gyllenhaal

■ FAVOURITE ACTIVITY ON DAY OFF

Spending time with my wife and child

■ FAVOURITE MUSICIAN / BAND

Orelsan – French rapper

■ POST-MATCH ROUTINE

I just try to switch off

■ BEST FRIEND IN FOOTBALL

That's difficult as I have so many! But probably Umut Bozok who plays for Trabzonspor

■ BIGGEST CAREER INFLUENCE

Probably my parents – they pushed me from a young age

■ PERSONAL LIFE AMBITION

When I started playing it was to play first division football in France – but the highest level is the Premier League, so I'll say that

■ IF YOU WEREN'T A FOOTBALLER, WHAT WOULD YOU BE

I really don't know!

■ PERSON IN WORLD YOU'D MOST LIKE TO MEET

Again, Jake Gyllenhaal!

YOU ARE THE REF

It wouldn't be a QPR Annual without this favourite feature, would it? Once again, you can take charge and solve our latest ten refereeing conundrums...

1 You order a penalty kick to be retaken. The player who took the first kick refuses to take it again, so his captain nominates another player to retake the kick. Do you allow this?

2 At a corner kick the goalkeeper stands in front of an opposing attacker and holds his arm out across that player to stop him getting forward to the ball. What do you do?

3 A penalty hits a post and comes straight back out to the penalty taker. The goalkeeper is on his back and the penalty taker is about to score the rebound but at that moment he is brought down in the area by a defender. What do you decide?

4 A defender takes a goal kick for his 'keeper but he miskicks it and it barely travels outside the area, he then rushes forward and kicks it properly up field. Is this allowed?

5

As a player is about to take a penalty an opposing player yells, "MISS IT!" and the taker is subsequently put off and misses the penalty. What action is required?

6

A defender uses his team-mate's shoulders to gain extra height before heading the ball away. What happens now?

7

As a referee you are making sure that the corner flags are the correct minimum height before a match. What should that minimum height be?

8

At half-time a team captain enters your dressing room and uses abusive language against you over a first-half decision. What action do you take?

9

After a strong run a winger centres the ball but his speed takes him over the goal-line near the corner flag. The ball is headed back in his direction by an opponent. The winger then runs back on the pitch and regains possession. Do you allow this?

10

A 'keeper rushes forward and collects the ball on the edge of his area but a defender is also rushing to help and has clattered into him, knocking him forward outside the area, still holding the ball. What do you do now?

Answers on **page 61**

THE BIG QPR QUIZ

The 2023/24 season was a breathless one for the R's. Question is – how much of it do you remember?

Take our bumper quiz to find out!

1. QPR started off the season with a rearranged fixture against which club?

2. The R's signed off the 2023/24 season with a 2-1 away win at which club?

3. Who were the four goalscorers in the thrashing of play-off contenders Leeds United on a memorable April evening?

4. Which player wore the number 11 shirt during the '23/24 campaign?

5. Which four players came into the club in the January transfer window?

6. Michael Frey scored a late equaliser at home to which club during the 2023/24 season?

7. The R's recorded their first home win of the season against which club?

8. Who scored QPR's first competitive goal of the last campaign?

You can check your answers on page 61

48

9 Which player received the first red card of the season in a home game versus Sunderland back in September?

10 QPR's second red card of the season was rescinded, but which player was this in relation to?

11 Who wore the number 37 shirt for the '23/24 season?

12 Which player scored twice against his old club in an evening match in March 2024?

13 Who made the most appearances during the 2023/24 season for the R's?

14 Which R's defender scored 'goal of the season' with a spectacular late strike against Birmingham City?

15 Which player made their competitive QPR first-team debut in the final game of the season?

16 One QPR player scored a super equaliser at home to Leicester before being sent off shortly afterwards, name that player.

17 Name the player who scored the Super Hoops' final goal of the last campaign.

18 Name the assistant to head coach Martí Cifuentes.

THE BIG QPR QUIZ

25 What nationality is Ziyad Larkeche?

26 Which international made his full R's debut away at West Brom in October 2023?

19 Which squad number did youngster Rayan Kolli wear during '23/24?

20 Who was the front-of-shirt sponsor for the first team during the season?

27 Who won the QPR players' player of the season?

28 Who won the fans' player of the season?

21 Which three colours were worn by the QPR goalkeeper over the course of the season?

29 QPR did the double over which Lancashire club?

30 How many clean sheets did the Hoops manage last season?

22 The away kit was celebrating an anniversary, the first time the 'Dennis the Menace' strip was worn. How many years ago was its first appearance? 30 years, 40 years or 50 years?

31 Who were joint-top scorers during 2023/24?

32 How many red cards did we receive last season?

23 What was the score when the boys from W12 won away at league leaders Leicester City in March 2024?

33 How many yellow cards were issued against us?

24 Who played in the number 22 shirt for the '23/24 campaign?

Answers on **page 61**

34 Which player received the most yellow cards?

35 How many wins did we manage during '23/24?

36 What was the final points total for 2023/24?

37 How many goals did we score for the season?

38 What was the final league position attained by the R's for the '23/24 season?

39 What was the highest attendance at Loftus Road during the last campaign? Was it a. 17,385, b. 17,745, c. 17,831 or d. 17,992?

40 Who were the opponents for the highest home attendance of the season?

41 Who were the opponents who inflicted the heaviest home defeat on us last season?

42 Who were the Premier League side who came from two goals down to win 3-2 at Loftus Road in the FA Cup?

43 Which loanee netted on his QPR debut away at Blackburn in a 2-1 win?

44 How many matches did Martí Cifuentes manage QPR for during the season following his arrival at the club?

45 Who made 22 appearances last season from the bench?

46 Name the player with the most assists, 10 in total for the season.

47 Isaac Hayden joined the Hoops on loan from which Premier League club?

48 What was the longest winning run by QPR during the season, 2, 3 or 4?

49 Name boss Martí Cifuentes' last club before joining QPR. Was it a. Hammarby, b. AaB or c. Sandefjord?

50 Who wore squad number 19 at QPR last term?

YOUR FINAL SCORE

/ 50

LEGENDS
OF THE LOFT

The legends of the Loft wall was created when supporters backed the renaming of the Ellerslie Road Stand as The Stanley Bowles Stand in 2022, while also highlighting their desire for other former R's greats to be recognised.

On the back of this, the club asked fans to select their top five QPR players, excluding Bowles. From the many thousands of votes received from supporters of all ages, the 10 Legends of the Loft were named as:

1   GERRY FRANCIS
2   ALAN MCDONALD
3   RODNEY MARSH
4   LES FERDINAND
5   ADEL TAARABT
6   KEVIN GALLEN
7   DAVE THOMAS
8   PHIL PARKES
9   RAY WILKINS
10 CLINT HILL

The Legends of the Loft artwork in the Loftus Engineering Stand was officially unveiled by Gerry Francis – who topped the poll – on Saturday 19th August 2023 when QPR hosted Ipswich Town in the first home league match of the 2023/24 season.

GERRY FRANCIS

QPR Career: 1969-79 & 1981-82
Appearances: **354**
Goals: **65**

Gerry Francis is one of the club's most successful individuals, both as a player and as a manager.

As a player, he made his first-team debut at the age of 17 in a First Division match against Liverpool.

He came through the successful youth team of the 1960s and went on to become captain of the England national team. Gerry remains the only QPR player to achieve this.

He captained arguably our greatest-ever side, the 1975/76 team that finished runners-up in the top-flight, missing out on the title to Liverpool by a solitary point. It was an achievement which gave the club our first taste of European football the following season.

Gerry won 12 England caps, eight of them as captain. These all came while he was a QPR player.

As a manager, he led the 1992/93 team to a fifth-place finish in the inaugural Premier League. Gerry was inducted into The Forever R's Club – our former players' association – on April 17th 2017.

ALAN MCDONALD

QPR Career: **1983-97**
Appearances: **483**
Goals: **18**

Alan McDonald made nearly 500 appearances for the Super Hoops spanning a 17-year period.

The Belfast-born centre-half, who would go on to be a crowd favourite at Loftus Road, originally signed for Rangers as a schoolboy following a trial in 1979. He signed schoolboy forms two years later and went on to make his first-team debut at Wolves in a First Division match in September 1983.

In his time as a player, 'Macca' led the R's to the 1986 League Cup final, in what was a memorable run to Wembley.

He scored an extra-time goal in our replay win over Chelsea in the quarter-finals, before QPR beat Liverpool in the semis. Rangers were unfortunately defeated by Oxford United in the final.

Macca also featured in a number of other famous R's victories, including a certain 6-0 win over Chelsea on Easter Monday of 1986, as well as a 4-1 drubbing of Manchester United at Old Trafford on New Year's Day in 1992.

He was part of the Rangers side that finished as the Premier League's top London club at the end of 1992/93 campaign.

The former Northern Irish skipper also won 52 international caps for his country. He is the most-capped player in the history of QPR.

After finishing his playing career at Swindon Town, he would eventually return to football – and Loftus Road – when he joined the club as then-boss Gary Waddock's assistant in 2006.

He later led Glentoran to the Irish League championship in 2009.

Macca sadly passed away on June 23rd 2012 at the age of 48. He was posthumously inducted into The Forever R's Club on February 11th 2017.

RODNEY MARSH

QPR Career: 1966-72
Appearances: 242
Goals: 134

Rodney Marsh signed for Rangers from Fulham in March 1966 for £15,000.

He made his debut that month at Peterborough and from that moment on, the course of the club's fortunes took an upward turn.

Rodney was part of the team that won the League Cup at Wembley Stadium in 1967 against West Brom, getting on the scoresheet as QPR came back from 2-0 down to win 3-2 – and doing so as a Third Division side against the top-flight Baggies.

Rodney also broke the club record for goals scored in a single season with a staggering 44 in all competitions as we won the Third Division title in 1966/67.

He also became QPR's first full England international in 63 years when he came on as a substitute against Switzerland at Wembley in November 1971.

Rodney is fourth on the club's all-time scoring list in all competitions.

He was inducted into The Forever R's Club on March 23rd 2017.

LES FERDINAND

QPR Career: 1987-95
Appearances: 183
Goals: 90

Having signed from non-league Hayes in 1987, Les Ferdinand's first-team chances were limited and he was loaned to Turkish side Besiktas.

On his return, though, under the management of first Don Howe and then Gerry Francis, Les developed into a high-quality striker.

In the 1992/93 season, Les scored 20 Premier League goals, form which earned him the first of seven England caps while a QPR player.

During that season he also became the first – and to date only – player in the club's history to score hat-tricks in consecutive matches when he plundered three at home to Nottingham Forest on April 10th 1993, and did so again at Everton just two days later.

Manager Francis would later put his own position on the line as he sought to keep Les at the club, fearing for the club's top-flight safety were he to be sold.

Les joined Newcastle United in the summer of 1995, and the R's suffered relegation the following season.

He was inducted into The Forever R's Club on October 15th 2016.

ADEL TAARABT

QPR Career: 2009-15
Appearances: 164
Goals: 34

Adel Taarabt initially joined QPR on loan from Tottenham for the final two months of the 2008/09 campaign before a season-long loan in 2009/10.

An incredibly-gifted individual, it was after he made the move from north London to west

London permanent in the summer of 2010 that the Moroccan would become an undeniable fans' favourite.

With Neil Warnock as his gaffer, Adel enjoyed a scintillating campaign in 2010/11, captaining the side to Championship glory and a return to the Premier League after a 15-year exile.

He scored 19 goals – including some absolute crackers – and contributed 16 assists as he was named the 2010/11 Football League Player of the Year.

Adel was also voted into the Championship's PFA Team of the Year and has gone down as one of the finest players to ever play in England's second tier.

In our first season back in the top-flight, QPR escaped certain relegation by winning our final five home fixtures. That included a 2-1 win over Arsenal and a 1-0 victory against Spurs. Adel netted in both matches.

KEVIN GALLEN

QPR Career:
1994-2000 & 2001-07
Appearances: 403
Goals: 97

A boyhood QPR fan from Acton, Kevin Gallen broke all manner of records for the youth team, scoring a remarkable 152 goals in 110 matches at that level between 1991 and 1994.

Kevin made his first-team debut away to Manchester United on August 20th 1994 at the age of 18.

He would go on to form a lethal partnership with Les Ferdinand in the Premier League. They netted 34 goals between them in 1994/95.

He left in 2000 for Huddersfield and then moved to Barnsley, but he returned to a hero's welcome in November 2001.

In his second spell in W12, Kevin helped rebuild the club after a spell in administration.

In 2002/03, Kevin scored 14 goals in all competitions as the R's reached the League One play-off final, losing in agonising fashion to Cardiff City.

The following season, Kevin was again as reliable as ever in front of goal, netting 17 in all competitions as QPR won promotion back to the Championship.

Kevin was inducted into The Forever R's Club on October 15th 2016.

DAVE THOMAS

QPR Career: 1972-77
Appearances: 220
Goals: 33

Dave Thomas remains one of the most popular players to have ever represented QPR.

He played a major role in a period of success – most notably the 1975/76 campaign which saw the Super Hoops being pipped to the league title by Liverpool on the final day of the campaign.

Having begun his career with Burnley, winger Thomas made over 150 appearances at Turf Moor, scoring 19 goals during the late 1960s and early 70s before he headed south in 1972.

Loftus Road would be Thomas' destination for a then-club record transfer fee and he would quickly make his debut in Rangers' victory over Sunderland a few days later.

Between 1972 and 1977, Dave could be seen distinctively running down the wing at Loftus Road with his socks rolled down. His speed and excellent crossing earned him eight England caps while at Rangers.

Dave was inducted into The Forever R's Club in 2017.

PHIL PARKES

QPR Career: 1970-79

Appearances: 406

Phil Parkes joined Rangers from Walsall in the summer of 1970.

He very quickly joined the ranks of all-time great QPR goalkeepers, along with the likes of Reg Allen and Peter Springett.

His performances were also rewarded with a full England cap earned in Lisbon, Portugal in April 1974.

Phil was an ever-present in 1975/76 when we came so close to winning the Division One title..

Despite the incredible talents of that side, it highlights just how well-regarded Phil was by the QPR faithful that he was named QPR player of the season for that campaign.

Phil was inducted into The Forever R's Club on October 15th 2016.

RAY WILKINS

QPR Career: 1989-96

Appearances: 215

Goals: 11

Ray Wilkins joined QPR on a free transfer from Glasgow Rangers in December 1989.

Many pundits thought his impact may be limited at the age of 33, but he went on to make a total of 207 appearances for the R's and scored 10 goals.

He was outstanding for the club, playing a key role in our success in the early 1990s and the emergence of players such as Les Ferdinand and Andy Sinton.

His form was so good, in fact, that there was even talk of an England recall.

After moving away for a short spell at Crystal Palace, Wilkins returned to Loftus Road as our player-manager in November 1994.

Rangers finished eighth in the Premier League that season.

He set a record as QPR's oldest-ever outfield player when he appeared versus Bolton Wanderers on September 1st 1996 at the age of 39 years, 352 days.

He was inducted into the Forever R's Club on October 28th 2016.

Ray sadly passed away on April 4th 2018 at the age of 61.

CLINT HILL

QPR Career: 2010-2016

Appearances: 185

Goals: 5

Clint Hill joined QPR from Crystal Palace in July 2010, teaming up with Neil Warnock who he had worked with at Selhurst Park.

The defender made an immediate impression. His no-nonsense defending and heart-on-sleeve attitude made him a real favourite with the Loftus Road faithful.

In his debut campaign in W12, Clint made 44 league appearances and was an integral part of our success as we won the 2010/11 Championship title.

The following season – our first in the top-flight for 15 years – QPR defied the odds to achieve survival in the Premier League on the final day.

Hill's never-say-die attitude was once again crucial to our success, and this was recognised as he picked up both the Supporters' and Players' Player of the Season accolades.

During the 2012/13 season, Clint was handed the club captaincy.

Despite relegation, Clint remained at the club and retained the skipper's armband as we achieved an immediate return to the top-flight with a play-off final victory over Derby County at Wembley Stadium.

He later described holding aloft the Championship play-off trophy in front of 40,000 R's fans as one of the proudest moments of his career.

Clint was inducted into The Forever R's Club on October 28th 2019.

FOCUS ON
LUCAS
ANDERSEN

■ **NATIONALITY**

Denmark

■ **POSITION**

Midfielder

■ **MARRIED**

No

■ **CHILDREN**

Yes, two

■ **CAR**

Right now, I don't
have one!

▪ FAVOURITE TV PROGRAMME

Suits

▪ FAVOURITE PLAYER IN WORLD FOOTBALL

Kevin De Bruyne

▪ MOST PROMISING TEAM-MATE

Daniel Bennie

▪ FAVOURITE 'OTHER' TEAM

AaB Aalborg

▪ CHILDHOOD FOOTBALLING HERO

Kaká or Ronaldinho

▪ FAVOURITE SPORT OTHER THAN FOOTBALL

Padel

▪ MOST DIFFICULT OPPONENT SO FAR (PLAYER)

As a team, Barcelona in a Champions League group stage game – take your pick of the players, Iniesta, Neymar, Messi!

▪ MOST MEMORABLE MATCH OF YOUR CAREER

Playing Barca at the Camp Nou in that game

▪ BIGGEST DISAPPOINTMENT SO FAR

Losing two cup Finals

▪ FAVOURITE MEAL

Italian

▪ FAVOURITE HOLIDAY DESTINATION

Italy

▪ FAVOURITE ACTIVITY ON DAY OFF

Being together with the family

▪ FAVOURITE MUSICIAN / BAND

Loyal Carner

▪ POST-MATCH ROUTINE

Grab something to eat with family

▪ BEST FRIEND IN FOOTBALL

Rasmus Thelander

▪ BIGGEST CAREER INFLUENCE

My first youth coach

▪ PERSONAL LIFE AMBITION

Pass on my knowledge and passion to the next in line in my family

▪ IF YOU WEREN'T A FOOTBALLER, WHAT WOULD YOU BE

A creative

▪ PERSON IN WORLD YOU'D MOST LIKE TO MEET

Probably Kaká or Ronaldinho to discuss their style and what they were thinking on the pitch

8
Sam
Field

Midfielder

England

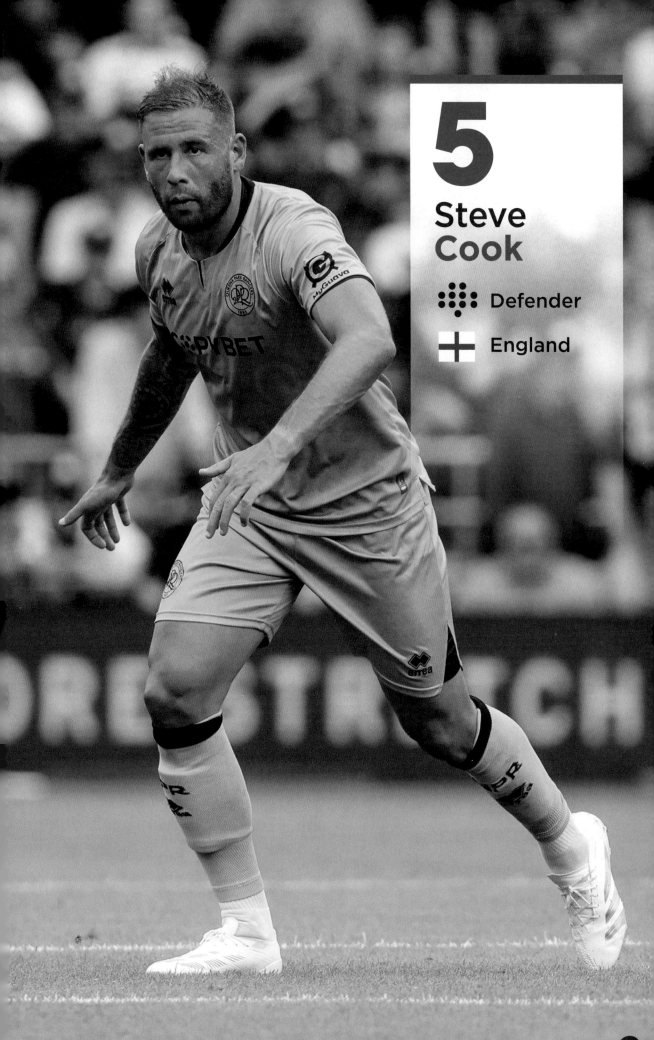

5

**Steve
Cook**

Defender

England

ANSWERS

Page 38: Wordsearch

```
S E L N I W O R H T L L S K
L D O V E R H E A D K I C K
I I C E O A A R E N R O C R
D S L H I G H P R E S S O I
I N Y T L A N E P A L D Y T
N O E S L O W B L O C K E O
G V R F C P V R L K D D L C
T W O F R R R K U K I E B R
A L E L G E D L O K S D B E
C Y L L L R E C F G S I I D
K N O L B E N K P E E S R C
L I L N O D Y C I D N F D A
E Y R E D A E H E C T F R R
D R A C W O L L E Y K O S D
```

Page 40: Spot the Difference

Page 39:
Who Am I?

1. Elijah Dixon-Bonner

2. Michael Frey

3. Jimmy Dunne

4. Ilias Chair

5. Joe Walsh

Page 41: It's a Numbers Game

Paul Nardi
+ Joe Walsh
= 1+13 **(14)**

Jimmy Dunne +
Jack Colback
= 3+4 **(7)**

Steve Cook
+ Harrison Ashby
= 5+20 **(25)**

Kader Dembélé
+ Paul Smyth
= 7+11 **(18)**

Sam Field
+ Koki Saito
= 8+14 **(22)**

Michael Frey
+ Liam Morrison
= 12+16 **(28)**

Kenneth Paal
+ Žan Celar
= 22+18 **(40)**

Lucas Andersen
+ Elijah Dixon-Bonner
= 25+19 **(44)**

Alfie Lloyd +
Hevertton Santos
= 28+23 **(51)**

Jake Clarke-Salter
+ Jonathan Varane
= 6+40 **(46)**

Page 46-47: You are the Ref

1. Yes, you can allow a different penalty taker.

2. You should award a penalty kick against the goalkeeper.

3. Award another penalty but don't send the defender off as he hasn't denied a clear goalscoring opportunity. Had the attacker scored from the rebound he would have been penalised for touching the ball twice. However, if the defender's challenge was rash, you may caution him.

4. No, you must award an indirect free-kick.

5. Have the penalty retaken.

6. Caution the defender and award an indirect free-kick against him.

7. 5ft.

8. Refuse to let the player take any further part in the match.

9. Yes, you do.

10. Award the opposition a free-kick, but there's no need to send the goalkeeper off as it was unintentional and didn't prevent a goalscoring opportunity.

Page 48-51: The Big QPR Quiz

1. Watford
2. Coventry City
3. Ilias Chair, Lucas Andersen, Lyndon Dykes and Sam Field
4. Paul Smyth
5. Isaac Hayden, Joe Hodge, Michael Frey, Lucas Andersen
6. Norwich City
7. Stoke City, a 4-2 win on November 28th
8. Sinclair Armstrong away at Cardiff City in a 2-1 away win
9. Jack Colback
10. Asmir Begović away at Leeds United
11. Albert Adomah
12. Sam Field
13. Asmir Begović
14. Jimmy Dunne
15. Joe Walsh
16. Andre Dozzell
17. Morgan Fox
18. Xavi Calm
19. Number 38
20. Convivia
21. Pink, Orange & Charcoal
22. 40 years, first worn in 1983/84
23. 2-1 to the Super Hoops
24. Kenneth Paal
25. French
26. Reggie Cannon
27. Jake Clarke-Salter
28. Steve Cook
29. Preston North End
30. 13
31. Lyndon Dykes & Ilias Chair
32. 4
33. 95
34. Jack Colback with 13
35. 15
36. 56
37. 49
38. 17th
39. C. 17,831
40. Norwich City
41. Blackburn Rovers, 0-4
42. AFC Bournemouth
43. Joe Hodge
44. 33
45. Paul Smyth
46. Ilias Chair
47. Newcastle United
48. 3
49. A. Hammarby
50. Elijah Dixon-Bonner

FIXTURES

QPR's 2024/25
Sky Bet Championship schedule

OCTOBER	Opponents	Home/Away	Score
Tue 1	HULL CITY	H	
Sat 5	DERBY COUNTY	A	
Sat 19	PORTSMOUTH	H	
Tue 22	COVENTRY CITY	H	
Sat 26	BURNLEY	A	

NOVEMBER	Opponents	Home/Away	Score
Sat 2	SUNDERLAND	H	
Tue 5	MIDDLESBROUGH	H	
Sat 9	LEEDS UNITED	A	
Sat 23	STOKE CITY	H	
Wed 27	CARDIFF CITY	A	
Sat 30	WATFORD	A	

DECEMBER	Opponents	Home/Away	Score
Sat 7	NORWICH CITY	H	
Wed 11	OXFORD UNITED	H	
Sat 14	BRISTOL CITY	A	
Sat 21	PRESTON NORTH END	H	
Thu 26	SWANSEA CITY	A	
Sun 29	NORWICH CITY	A	

JANUARY	Opponents	Home/Away	Score
Wed 1	WATFORD	H	
Mon 6	LUTON TOWN	H	
Sat 18	PLYMOUTH ARGYLE	A	
Tue 21	HULL CITY	A	
Sat 25	SHEFFIELD WED	H	